black is brown is tan

Arnold Adoff

pictures by
Emily Arnold McCully

HarperCollinsPublishers

Amistad

for

leigh   and   jaime

black   and   t a n

kiss   big   sister

hug

big   m a n

black is brown is tan

Text copyright © 1973 by Arnold Adoff Text copyright renewed 2001 by Arnold Adoff
Illustrations copyright © 2002 by Emily Arnold McCully Printed in Singapore. All rights reserved.
www.harperchildrens.com

Library of Congress Cataloging-in-Publication Data
Adoff, Arnold.
    Black is brown is tan / by Arnold Adoff ; pictures by Emily Arnold McCully.
        p.   cm.
    Summary: Describes in poetic form a family with a brown-skinned mother, light-skinned father, two children, and
their various relatives.
    ISBN 0-06-028776-4 — ISBN 0-06-028777-2 (lib. bdg.)
    [1. Human skin color—Fiction.   2. Racially mixed people—Fiction.   3. Family life—Fiction.   4. Stories in
rhyme]   I. McCully, Emily Arnold, ill.   II. Title.
PZ8.3.A233 Bl   2002   00-011861
[E]—dc21

Typography by Matt Adamec
3 4 5 6 7 8 9 10
❖

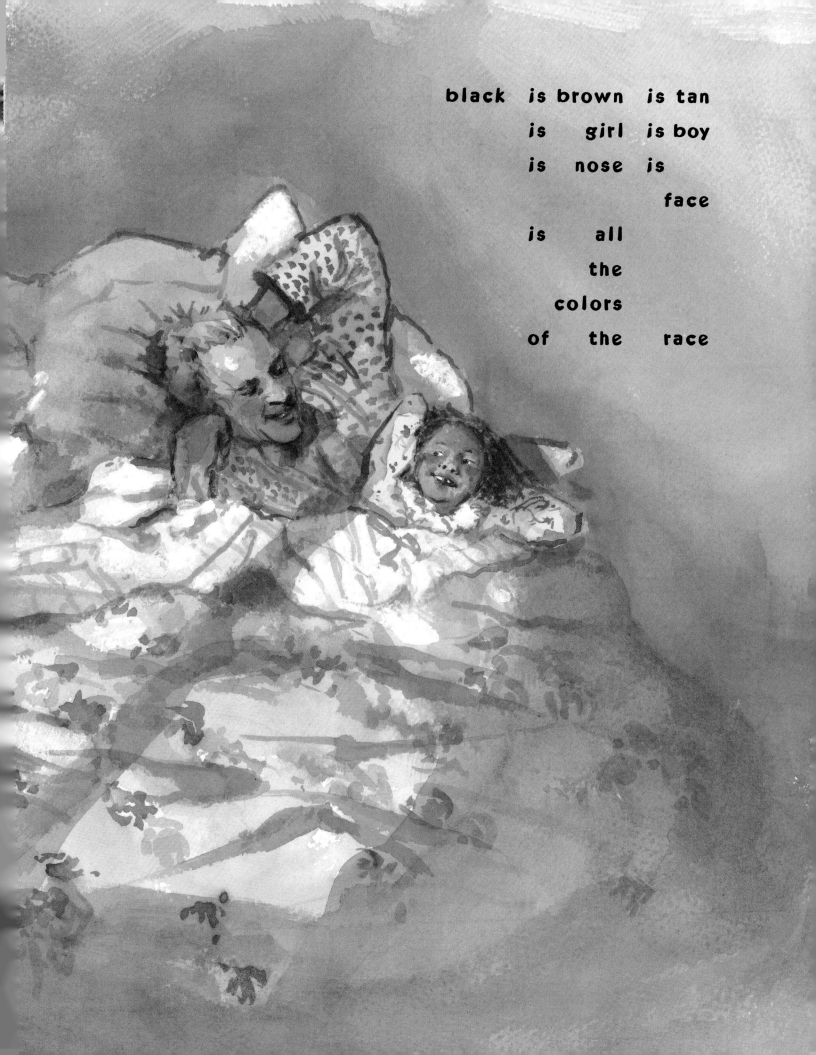

black *is* brown *is* tan
is girl *is* boy
is nose *is*
face
is all
the
colors
of the race

is dark   is light
singing   songs
in
singing   night

kiss big woman   hug big man
black   is   brown   is   tan

this is the way it is for us   this is the way we are

i am mom   am mommy   mama mamu   meeny muh
                                and   mom   again
with mighty hugs   and hairbrush mornings
                                catching   curls
later we sit by the window
and   your   head *is* up against   my chest
we read   and tickle   and   sing the words
                                into   the   a i r

go out   to cut wood   for the fire
or cook the corn and chicken legs

and you say   you getting bigger   than me
and you say   c h o c o l a t e   m o m m a
               c h o c o l a t e   u p
                                             t h e
                                             m i l k

and *i* say drink the milk
and l a u g h out loud

i am black   i am brown   the milk is chocolate   brown
i am the   c o l o r   of   the milk   chocolate   cheeks
                        and   h a n d s   that   darken
                        in   the   s u m m e r   sun

                        a nose that peels brown skin
                                                in
                        a u g u s t

i am black   i am   a   brown   sugar   gown
a   tasty   tan   and   coffee   pumpkin   pie
with   dark   brown   eyes   and   almond   ears
     and   my   f a c e   gets   ginger   red
     when i   puff   and   yell   you   into bed

this is the way it is for us   this is the way we are

i am dad   am daddy   dingbat da
and   k i s s   me   pa
with the   big   belly   and   the
loud   voice
sitting   at   my desk
and   you   sit   on   my lap
we   read   and laugh a n d   pinch
t h e   words
into   t h e a i r

go out   to cut wood   for the fire
or cook the   corn   and hamburgers

and you say   you getting bigger than me
when i say   d r i n k   t h e   m i l k

i am white   the milk   is white
i am not the color of the milk
i am white   the snow   is white
i am not the color of the snow

i am white i am white
i am light
with pinks   and   tiny tans
dark hair g r o w i n g on my arms
that d a r k e n in the summer sun

brown eyes
big yellow ears

and my f a c e gets tomato red
when i puff and yell you into bed

there *is* granny white   and grandma black
kissing both your cheeks
                    and hugging   back

sitting by the window   telling stories of ago

and you say you getting bigger than all of them

and pour a glass of milk for every one

black is brown is tan

is girl is boy

is nose is

face

is all

the

colors

of the race

kiss big woman   hug big man
black   is   brown   is   tan